MONEY MIDAS

SONIA CRADDOCK

MONEY MIDAS

illustrated by David Shaw

RED DEER COLLEGE PRESS

Northern Lights Books for Children are published by
Red Deer College Press
56 Avenue & 32 Street Box 5005
Red Deer Alberta Canada T4N 5H5

Edited for the Press by Tim Wynne-Jones
Designed by David Shaw & Associates Ltd.
Printed and bound in Korea for Red Deer College Press
Financial support provided by the Alberta Foundation
for the Arts, a beneficiary of the Lottery Fund of the
Government of Alberta, and by the Canada Council, the
Department of Communications and Red Deer College.

COMMITTED TO THE DEVELOPMENT OF CULTURE AND THE ARTS

Canadian Cataloguing in Publication Data

Craddock, Sonia.
  Money Midas

(Northern lights books for children)
ISBN 0-88995-113-6

I. Shaw, David, 1947- II. Title. III. Series.
PS8555.R24M6 1994 jC813'.54 C94-910147-8
PZ7.C72Mo 1994

For Michael

Sonia Craddock

For Flori and Holly

David Shaw

Mr. Midas was
the richest person in the
world.
     Mr. Midas had more
money than anyone else
in the whole world.
     People called him
Money Midas.

Oh, yes, Money Midas was rich. But was he happy? No, he wasn't. Money Midas didn't just want to be the richest person in the whole world. He wanted to own everything.

"I want to buy the whole world," he told his daughter, Goldy. Goldy was the only family he had, and Goldy was all he cared about—after money of course. But Goldy didn't care about money. She was much too busy reading to her pet monkey.

"I'm going to buy a wish," Money Midas told his daughter. "I'm going to buy a wish that will let me own everything in the whole world."

"I don't think you can buy a wish, Daddy Midas," said Goldy. Goldy had read a lot of stories and she knew about wishes.

"Hah! I can buy anything," said Money Midas. "I'm the richest person in the whole world." Money Midas hadn't read a story in a long time.

Right away he gathered all his workers together—more people worked for Money Midas than for anyone else in the whole world. "Get me the Wish Department!" he yelled. "Immediately!"

The Wish Department. Yes. The most closely guarded secret in the whole wide world. No one knows where it is. No one knows how to find it. No one knows who runs it, and no one knows what the Wishers look like. That's what they're called—Wishers. If farmers are people who grow crops, and bakers are people who bake bread, then Wishers are people who grant wishes. Don't we wish we knew who they are!

"Spare no expense," ordered Money Midas.

"Go! Search! Talk to everyone in the whole world—and don't stop until you find the Wishers."

The Money Midas men and the Money Midas women went north and south and east and west. They went up into the dark of outer space and down into the depths of the oceans. Day and night, night and day, they searched. But they didn't find anything. No sign of the Wishers anywhere.

Then Money Midas got all the newspapers and radio stations and TV networks from all over the world, and he ordered them to advertise for the Wishers twenty-four hours a day. No one got to see any programs or read any news. All they could see and hear and read was Money Midas's advertisement.

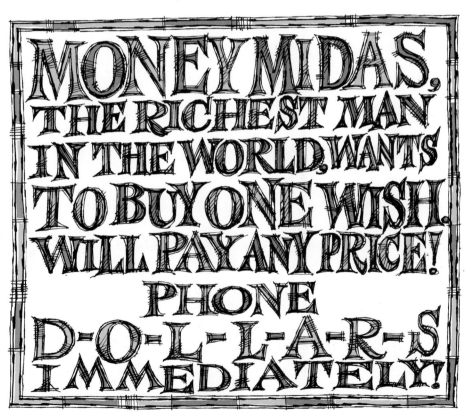

MONEY MIDAS, THE RICHEST MAN IN THE WORLD, WANTS TO BUY ONE WISH. WILL PAY ANY PRICE! PHONE D-O-L-L-A-R-S IMMEDIATELY!

Money Midas waited and waited. Dozens of people phoned D–O–L–L–A–R–S and said they could sell him a wish. But they were all pretending. They were all phonies.

"I wish those Wishers would hurry up and sell me my wish," Money Midas said to Goldy. "Don't they know what 'immediately' means?"

"I don't think money can buy wishes, Daddy Midas," said Goldy.

"Hah!" said Money Midas, and he picked up the phone. "Get me World Air!" he shouted. "And World Bus and World Train, too!"

Then Money Midas got all the travel companies in the whole world together and gave them billions of copies of his advertisement and told them to scatter it from their windows—all around the world. And so the planes and trains and buses and taxis all stopped taking passengers, and loaded up with Money Midas's advertisement instead. And no one could go anywhere.

Money Midas waited and waited and waited. Hundreds of people phoned, but they were all phonies and fakes.

"Those Wishers had better hurry up and sell me my wish," Money Midas said to Goldy.

"I know a wish you don't have to buy, Daddy Midas," said Goldy. "Let's wish we could go to the park!"

"No! No! That's not what I want," said Money Midas, and he picked up the phone. "Get me all the storekeepers in the world!" he shouted. "And all the traveling salespeople and all the people who have stalls at markets!"

Then Money Midas got all the storekeepers and all the traveling salespeople and all the market sellers together, and told them to sell nothing except his advertisement: no bread, no potatoes, no candy, no toys, no ice cream, no spinach, no cough syrup, no furniture, no microwaves, no soap—No Nothing!

And so nothing in the whole world was sold except Money Midas's advertisement. And no one could buy anything else.

Money Midas waited and waited and waited and waited! Thousands of people phoned, but they were all phonies, fakes and charlatans.

And what did the Wishers think about all this?

In the most secret place in the world, the Wishers were very worried.

"What shall we do about Money Midas?" asked the youngest Wisher. "No one can buy anything. No one can travel anywhere. No one can read or watch TV. The whole world has come to a stop!"

"We can't sell a wish," said the second youngest Wisher. "It's against all the rules. Money Midas might be the richest person in the world, but he still can't buy a wish."

"That's right," all the Wishers agreed.

"So we'll *give* him one," said the wisest Wisher. "We'll give Money Midas his wish."

"Give him a wish?" All the other Wishers were horrified. "Give him a wish? Just because he's the richest person in the world?"

"No, no," laughed the wisest Wisher. "I've been around for a long time. Wishes are tricky things. *Give* him his wish."

So they did.

And they sent the youngest Wisher in disguise to do the job.

The very next day, when Money Midas was on the phone to ten different places at once, an old woman hobbled into the room. She was bent and white haired and leaned on a stick.

"How did you get in here?" Money Midas waved her away. "Get out! Can't you see I'm busy?"

"Oh, kind sir. I just want to ask you for a crust of bread," the old woman said in a quavering voice.

"Crust of bread! Crust of bread!" Money Midas went red in the face. "Get out! Get out!" And he waved the old woman away.

The old woman sighed and sat down on a sofa. "I had hoped you'd earn your wish," she said. "This is the first wish I've ever given, and I just hate giving one to someone who doesn't deserve it."

"Wish?" Money Midas dropped the phone. "Did you say 'Wish'?"

"That's what I'm here for," said the old woman. "But I'm surprised you wouldn't give an old woman a crust of bread. You obviously haven't read many stories."

"How much do you want?" Money Midas reached for his wallet. "Name your price."

"There is no price," said the old woman. "We don't sell wishes. We're giving you one. It's free."

"But I'm the richest person in the world," said Money Midas. "I can afford a million—a billion—a trillion."

"There is no price on a wish," said the old woman again. "We don't sell wishes."

"A free wish?" Money Midas shook his head in surprise.

"Now," said the old woman, "I haven't got all day. Tell me your wish."

Money Midas stood up straight and cleared his throat. "This is my wish," he said. "I wish that everything I touch will turn to gold."

"Are you sure?" asked the old woman.

"Yes," said Money Midas, and he rubbed his hands. "The world will soon be mine!"

"Very well," said the old woman. "Your wish has just come true."

"Just like that?" asked Money Midas.

"Just like that," said the old woman.

Money Midas whirled around. He put out a hand and touched the big oak desk—and immediately it turned into solid gold.

"Gold! Gold!" Money Midas shouted. "My wish has come true." He whirled and twirled around the room—touching tables, chairs, stools, computers, curtains, books, papers, pictures, pens, pencils, erasers, hole punchers, rulers, vases, flowers, ornaments, until the room shone and flashed like a golden mirror and he was dizzy.

"And this is just the beginning!" he said. But the old woman had disappeared.

Then Money Midas whirled all through the high-rise palace— touching, touching, touching. He raced through the rooms—from the basement to the roof. And everything he touched turned to gold. He rushed and ran and raced—touching, touching, touching, until the whole high-rise was GOLD!

"What a wish!" he said. "By tomorrow I'll have enough gold to buy everything in the whole wide world." And he rang a golden bell for room service. "All this turning into gold has made me very hungry." And Money Midas flung himself into a golden chair and ordered a pizza and a large chocolate milkshake.

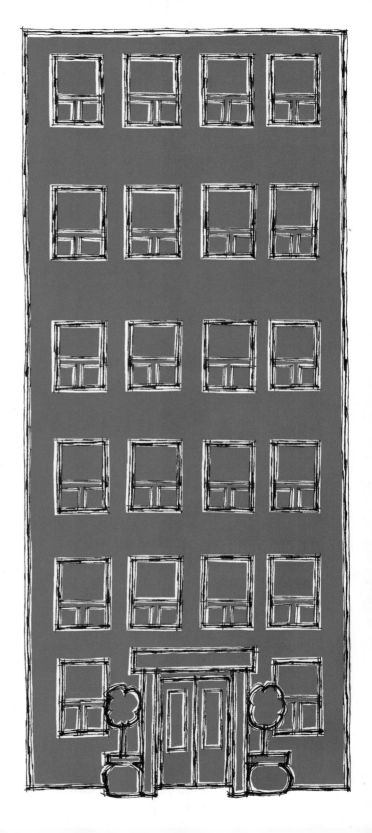

Money Midas was so hungry when the pizza came that he grabbed the biggest piece and stuffed it into his mouth . . . C–R–U–N–C–H!

His teeth bit down onto solid gold. The pizza had turned to gold: the pepperoni, mushrooms, pineapple, anchovies had all turned to gold!

Money Midas grabbed the chocolate milkshake, stuck the straw in his mouth and slurped a great slurp . . . C–L–A–N–G!

The chocolate milkshake had turned into gold.

Then Money Midas ordered hamburgers and spaghetti, hot dogs and macaroni and cheese. He ordered roast beef and ice cream, cake and popcorn, crackers and hot soup, cereal and porridge. He even ordered spinach and broccoli, even though he didn't like them—just in case.

But, you guessed it, everything turned instantly into gold!

Money Midas tried using different kinds of straws. He tried wearing

gloves and tipping soup from a jug into his mouth without touching it with his hands. He tried sneaking up fast on the food, and he tried putting the food into his mouth very, very slowly. He tried having a servant stand across the room and throw the food into his mouth. Nothing worked. Nothing. All that happened was that Money Midas got hungrier and hungrier and thirstier and thirstier.

"Oh, for a cold glass of water!" he cried. "If only I could eat a crust of bread."

And then, who should come running into the room but Goldy with her pet monkey.

"Daddy Midas," she called, running toward him. "Why is everything gold? My toys are all gold. Even my stuffed panda is gold. And my bed is gold, too. I wanted to go to sleep, but the golden pillow hurt my head."

When Money Midas
saw his daughter running
toward him, his heart
began to beat hard. "No!
No!" he cried. "Goldy!
Stay away from me!" And
he put his hands up to
stop her.

Too late. Goldy
rushed into his arms.
Instantly, she turned into
a golden statue. So did
the pet monkey.

Money Midas felt a pain around his heart and
tears came into his eyes. But he couldn't even cry. For
as soon as the tears came out, they changed to gold and
fell heavily onto his lap like golden coins.

"I'm the richest person in the world," Money Midas said to the golden statue, and he stacked the golden tears in piles. "I'll soon fix this." And he shouted into his golden phone. "Get me all the doctors in the world—immediately!"

And all the doctors in the world had to leave their patients and rush to the golden high-rise of Money Midas.

"I want you to bring my daughter back to life," he ordered, pointing at the golden statue.

But the doctors shook their heads. "There is nothing we can do," they said and hurried back to their patients.

Money Midas sat by the golden statue with his golden pizza and his golden milkshake—and the pile of golden tears grew higher and higher around him. CLANG! CLANG! went the golden tears as they hit the golden floor.

"I'm the richest person in the world!" Money Midas said to the golden statue. "I'll soon fix this." And he shouted into his golden phone. "Get me all the scientists in the world—immediately!"

All the scientists in the world had to leave their experiments and rush to the golden high-rise of Money Midas.

"Please bring my daughter back to life," he said.

But the scientists shook their heads. "There is nothing we can do," they said and hurried back to their experiments.

So Money Midas called for all the magicians and all the inventors and all the alchemists in the world. And they all came hurrying to the golden high-rise, and they all tried everything they could try. But nothing worked.

And Money Midas was so sad and so weak from not eating and drinking that he could hardly speak.

"What's the use of being the richest person in the world if I can never eat or drink again?" he groaned. "What's the use of owning everything in the world if my only daughter is a golden statue? Oh, I wish I hadn't made this wish."

There was a cough behind him, and when he turned around, there was the old woman leaning on her stick. "I was wondering if I could have a crust of bread?" she asked.

"Take everything you can find." Money Midas buried his face in his hands. "Anything."

"Ah . . . that's better," said the old woman, and she gave a little smile.

"If you'll take this wish away, I'll pay you all the money I have in the world," said Money Midas.

"We don't buy wishes," said the old woman. "We don't *sell* them, and we don't *buy* them."

"Ah," said Money Midas. "I guess not. But can you at least bring my little daughter, Goldy, back to life? If she hadn't loved me, she wouldn't have been turned into gold." And he wept more golden tears. CLANG! CLANG!

"If only I could have my wish all over again," said Money Midas. "I'd rather be the poorest person in the world and see my daughter as she used to be."

"Well," said the old woman. "I guess the wisest Wisher was right after all." And she banged her stick on the floor.

The sun shone down on the city streets. On the busiest corner stood a wooden bench. A man sat on the bench drinking a cup of water. A girl and her pet monkey sat next to him.

"I wish we could go to the park," said the girl. "We could sit under the trees and I could read you a story."

"Just what I was wishing," said the man. In the

pocket of his coat, he found a crust of bread. He broke it in two and gave half to the girl. She gave half of her piece to the monkey.

"Daddy," asked the girl, "do you miss being rich?"

"Hah!" said her father. He smiled and drained the very last drop of water from the cup.

"I'm the richest man in the world."